Whales

Written by
Jill Atkins

Contents

Are whales fish?	4
Whales with teeth	6
Whales without teeth	10
A pod of whales	13
Whale talk	14
Hunting for whales	15
Other dangers	16
Whale watching	17
Where to find whales	18
Glossary	20

Are whales fish?

Whales live in the oceans and seas all over the world.

They are not fish. They are mammals. This means that their blood is warm.

They don't lay eggs like fish; they have babies.

Calves

Did you know? A baby whale is called a calf. The calves feed on their mother's milk for many months, even up to two years. A calf stays near its mother until it is almost an adult.

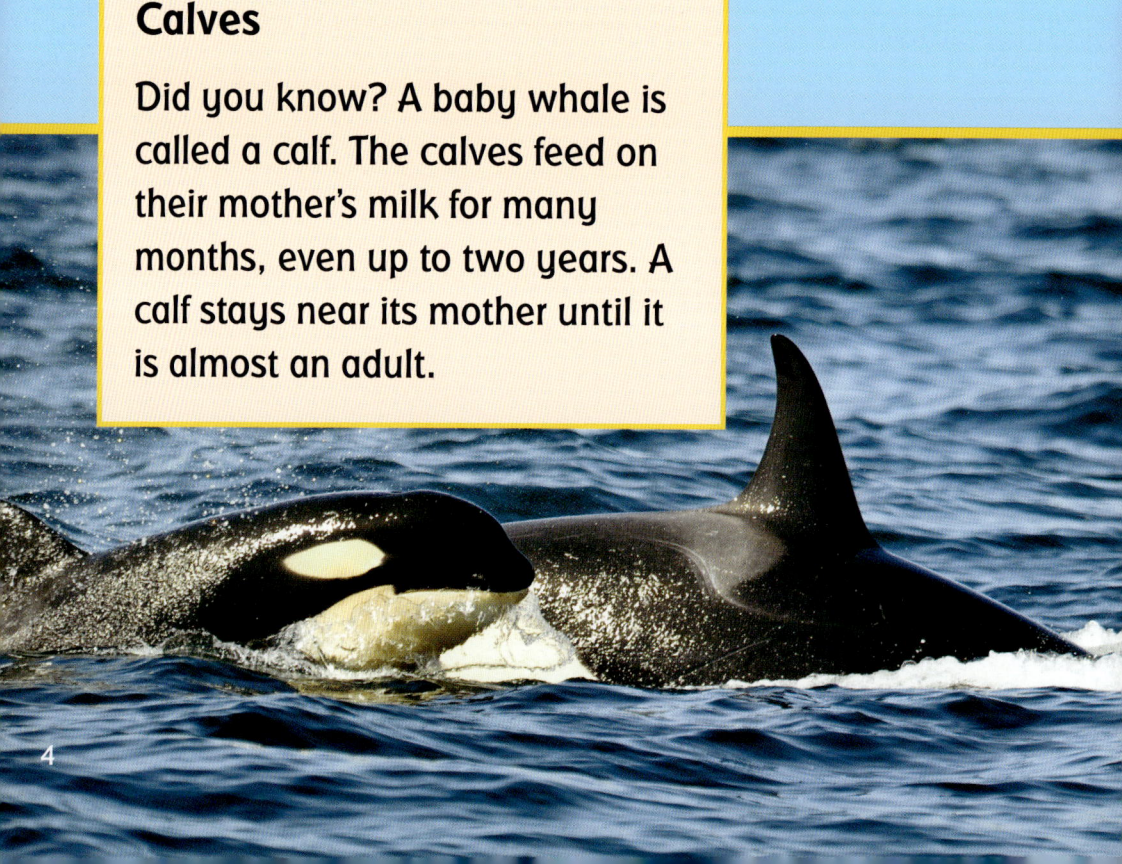

Blow-hole

A whale can't breathe under water like fish can.

It has to come up to the surface of the water to breathe. The whale breathes through a hole in its head called a blow-hole.

Whales with teeth

Some whales have sharp teeth.
They eat fish and other sea creatures.
Here are some of them:

1   Orca

The fiercest whale is the killer whale. It is also called an orca.

Killer whales eat fish, seals, squid, penguins and dolphins. They even kill the calves of other kinds of whales.

In the wild, killer whales are very fierce, but some are kept in a sea life centre. They can become very friendly with humans. Sometimes they learn to perform tricks.

2   Beluga

The white whale is called the beluga. It lives in the cold waters of the Arctic Ocean.

Beluga whales eat small fish, shellfish, squid and octopus.

An adult beluga is only about 5 metres long.

Fascinating fact

A beluga calf is dark grey. It will slowly become white.

3   Narwhal

A narwhal is a small whale. It is not much bigger than a dolphin. Narwhals eat small fish and shellfish.

Fascinating fact

The male narwhal grows a long tusk. This tusk is sometimes 3 metres long.

Sometimes two male narwhals have tusk fights over a female.

Four male narwhals

Whales without teeth

Some whales have no teeth. These are known as baleen whales. They have a kind of filter in their mouths. The filter is like a fine brush.

Baleen whales scoop up water into their mouths. Then they filter out hundreds of tiny sea creatures called krill to eat.

1 Blue whale

The blue whale is a kind of baleen whale. It is also the biggest whale. It can be as long as 30 metres.

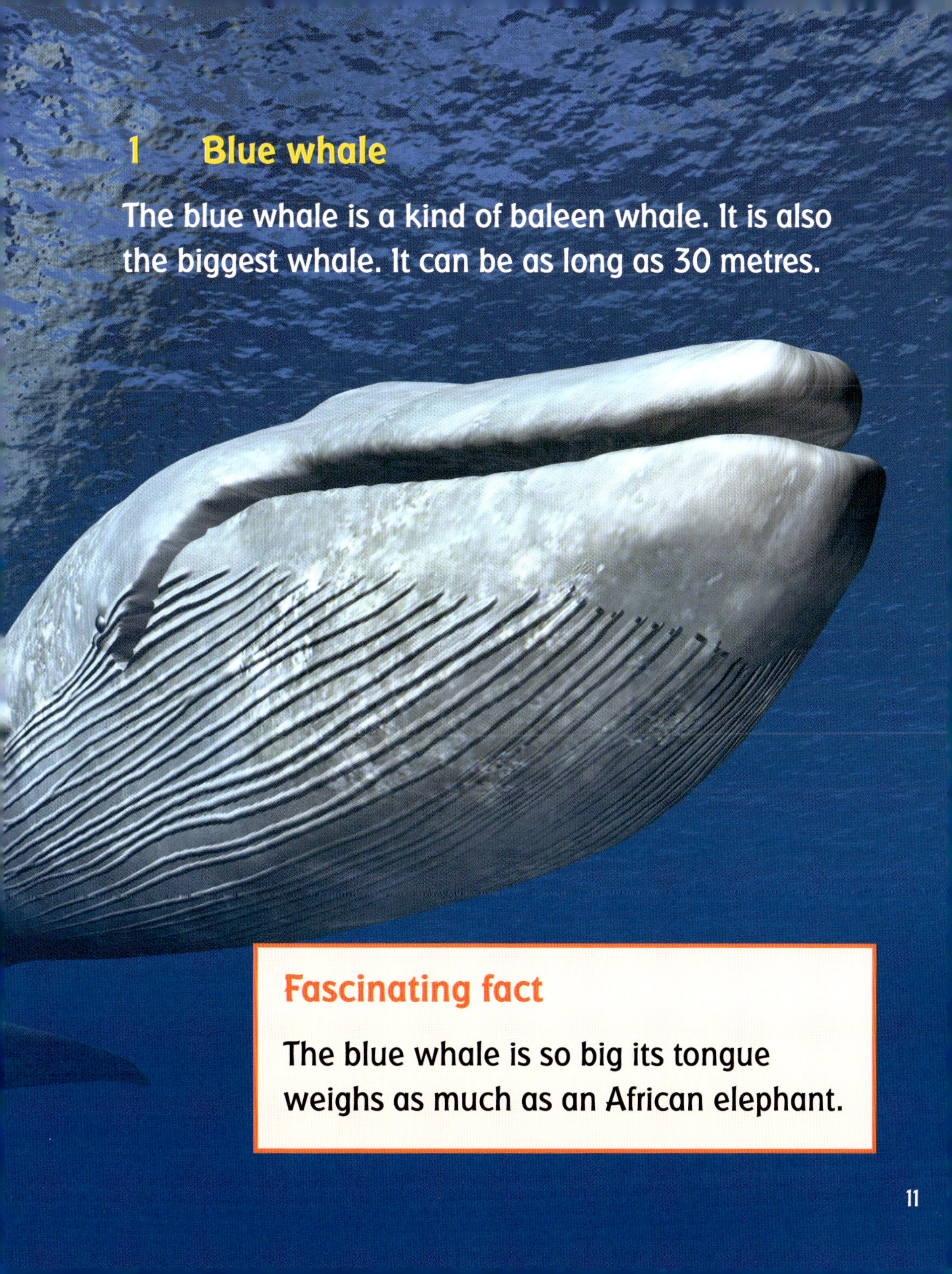

Fascinating fact

The blue whale is so big its tongue weighs as much as an African elephant.

2   Other baleen whales

There are many other kinds of baleen whales:
- right whales
- grey whales
- humpback whales
- minke whales.

A humpback whale

A pod of whales

A group of whales is called a pod. A pod is almost always members of one family.

A pod of killer whales

The whales with teeth often keep together in a pod. They look after each other and hunt together.

Baleen whales do not stay in a pod. They like to be alone or with one or two other whales.

Whale talk

Whales 'talk' with each other a lot. Different whales make different noises.

The baleen whales make deep grunts and snores. They use these to make echoes under the water.

The whales with teeth make high sounds. They make clicks and whistles.

Belugas make sounds like singing.

Beluga whales

Hunting for whales

Whales face many dangers. Their biggest danger is from hunters.

Why do hunters kill whales?

- Sometimes a whale is killed for its blubber. This is a kind of fat that can be used for candles and lamps. It can also be used to make soap and even lipstick!
- Whales are also killed for meat.
- Some baleen whales are killed for their bones.

An old whaling ship

Because of this, some whale species are almost extinct.

There is now a ban on whaling, but some countries still hunt them.

Other dangers

- Whales can be poisoned by pollution in the sea.

Sea pollution

- They can also die if they are caught in big fishing nets.

- Whales can get stuck on a beach at low tide. Sometimes they go back to sea on a high tide.

A whale stuck on a beach

Whale watching

People like to watch whales.

- Some people go to see them in 'sea world' centres.
- Some people go out in boats and watch whales out at sea.
- Some people watch whales on television or on the internet.

Watching whales at sea

Where to find whales

	Killer whales
	Humpback whales
	Beluga whales
	Blue whales
	Narwhals

Glossary

baleen whale	kind of whale without teeth
beluga	small white whale
blow-hole	hole that whales use to breathe
blubber	fat under a whale's skin
blue whale	kind of baleen whale
calf	baby whale
humpback whale	kind of baleen whale
mammal	animal where babies are born alive and the mother feeds them with her milk
narwhal	small whale with a long, pointed spear-like tusk
orca	another name for the killer whale
pod	name for a group of whales
pollution	oil and rubbish in the sea, land or air. It can kill plants and animals.